FIELD TRIP MYSTERIES

The **YELLOWSTONE** Kidnapping That Wasn't

by
Steve Brezenoff

illustrated by
Marcos Calo

STONE ARCH BOOKS
a capstone imprint

Field Trip Mysteries are published by Stone Arch Books
A Capstone Imprint
1710 Roe Crest Drive
North Mankato, Minnesota 55603
www.capstonepub.com

Library of Congress Cataloging-in-Publication Data
Brezenoff, Steven.
The Yellowstone kidnapping that wasn't / by Steve Brezenoff ;
illustrated by Marcos Calo.
p. cm. -- (Field trip mysteries)
ISBN 978-1-4342-3789-7 (library binding) -- ISBN 978-1-4342-
4200-6 (pbk.)
1. School field trips--Juvenile fiction. 2. Kidnapping--
Juvenile fiction. 3. Yellowstone National Park--Juvenile
fiction. [1. School field trips--Fiction. 2. Kidnapping--
Fiction. 3. Yellowstone National Park--Fiction. 4. Mystery
and detective stories.] I. Calo, Marcos, ill. II. Title.
III. Title: Yellowtone kidnapping that was not. IV. Series:
Brezenoff, Steven. Field trip mysteries.
PZ7.B7576Yel 2012
813.6--dc23   2012000048

Graphic Designer: Kay Fraser

Summary: When Samantha "Sam" Archer and her
friends in the nature club arrive in Yellowstone
Park on a school trip, they find that the park
superintendent's son may have been kidnapped.

Printed in the United States of America in
Stevens Point, Wisconsin.
032012   006678WZF12

TABLE OF CONTENTS

Samantha Archer

A.K.A: Sam

D.O.B: August 20th

POSITION: 6th Grade

Why are these kids so interested in field trips? I will look into this!

INTERESTS:

Old movies, (field trips)

KNOWN ASSOCIATES:

Duran, Catalina; Garrison, Edward; and Shoo, James.

NOTES:

Samantha frequently uses expressions many of the students—and even some of the teachers—do not understand. These seem to come from the old movies she watches at home.

Samantha recently called me Mr. Spade's "Bruno." What does this mean? I will look into this, too.

CHAPTER ONE

YELLOWSTONE

While I walked, my bag kept sliding off my shoulders.

I felt worse for my friend Egg, though.

He's smaller than I am, and his bag was much heavier.

"Honestly, Egg," I said. "Did you have to bring all that stuff?"

"Yellowstone National Park has some of the most beautiful scenery in the world, Sam," he said. "I'd regret it if I didn't bring all my equipment." His camera equipment, that is. I don't get his obsession with photography. Still, his pictures sometimes come in handy when we're investigating a mystery.

"I hope we see a moose," Cat said. Her name is short for Catalina, like my name — Sam — is short for Samantha.

"I hope we don't see a bear," added Gum, the fourth mystery-solver. His name is really James Shoo. Long story.

Of course we all knew we'd end up seeing a bear. It was the main reason most of the kids in the nature club had voted to go to Yellowstone National Park for our trip.

Gum had voted for the local petting zoo.

Gum walked next to me with his bag in one hand and his sleeping bag rolled up and strapped to his back. He blew a bubble. "I have never heard of anyone getting mangled by a baby goat," he said.

"A kid," Egg said.

"What kid?" Gum asked, shocked. "A kid got mangled by a baby goat?!"

Egg shook his head. "A kid is a baby goat," he said.

"There's a kid who's a baby goat?" Gum said. "Where did you read that? You can't believe everything you read on the internet, Egg."

Cat and I laughed. Sometimes it was hard to tell when Gum was joking, but he always made us laugh.

"Anyway, Mr. Neff told us how to deal with a bear encounter," Cat said. "I just hope you were paying attention."

Gum nodded. He reached down to his belt and pulled off a big bell. Then he clanked it up and down, so it rang loud and clear. "Here we come, bears!" he shouted. "Clear a path, please!"

"That's a good start," Cat said. "But what if we do meet a bear?"

Gum shook his head. "I'm just going to hope we don't," he said.

"Well, I think we're safe for now," I said. "Since we're still in the parking lot."

"Oh yeah," Gum said. "Good point."

Up ahead, Mr. Neff and the rest of the nature club stopped in front of the main park building. We caught up and gathered around.

I spotted Anton Gutman across the group from me. He was standing with his two goon friends. They were standing in a tight little circle, cackling about something.

"We're going to check in now," Mr. Neff said. "Ms. Harrison and I —"

"Garrison," said Ms. Garrison. That's Egg's mom — she was the chaperone on this trip. She looked just like Egg: very short. She was even wearing glasses and a sweater vest, just like Egg.

"What did I say?" Mr. Neff asked. He always got everyone's names wrong.

"You said Harrison," she said, smiling.

Mr. Neff went on, "Ms. Garrison and I will go sign in. We'll get our campsite assignment, and then we'll start our hike."

"What do the rest of us do?" Gum asked.

"Feel free to look around, but don't wander off," Mr. Neff said. He and Egg's mom went inside the main building.

Seconds later, Anton and his goons were standing in front of us.

"Hello, dorks," Anton said. His friends laughed. Anton stepped up to Gum. He just stared at Gum for a couple of seconds. Then, suddenly, he threw up his arms and growled in Gum's face, like a big, ugly bear.

Gum flinched. Anton's goons laughed and laughed. "Let's go inside," I said. "Something stinks out here."

"Yeah, you!" Anton said. His goons laughed some more.

My friends and I went inside the main building. "Don't worry about those jerks," Egg said.

"He didn't scare me," Gum said. "He just surprised me."

The four of us wandered down the hall of the main building. Soon we came to the office of the park superintendent. I peeked inside.

The park superintendent was at her desk. Across the desk from her, standing up and screaming, was a boy. He looked about fifteen, and he was mad.

"I told you I wanted a GameStation!" he screamed.

"Hollis," said the woman at the desk, "we've been over this. You won't get a GameStation because you didn't keep your grades up." She was trying to stay calm, but she was upset. I guess it would be pretty embarrassing if you ran a big park like Yellowstone, and your son was shouting at you in the office.

"Let's keep moving," I whispered to my friends.

"Yeah," Cat said. "It's not polite to snoop."

"On personal stuff," Gum said. "When it's for solving a mystery, we snoop like crazy!"

We all laughed. Then we started walking off, but we could still hear the kid complaining in the office.

Down the hallway, I saw Mr. Neff. He was heading outside. "We better hurry," I said.

Just then, Anton came speeding around the corner. He practically knocked Cat right over. "Watch it, dorks," he said. Then he ran on down the hall.

"Mr. Neff is done signing us in!" Egg called after him. "It's time to go!"

Anton didn't answer.

We all got back on the bus. The bus was pulling away when, suddenly, the driver slammed on the brakes. The door swung open, and Anton climbed on, out of breath and smirking. He hurried to a seat in the middle, where his goons were saving him a spot. Finally, we pulled away.

The park is huge. It's beyond huge. It's almost three and a half thousand square miles, and it's in three different states. Getting to our campsite on foot would have been impossible.

We drove for another half hour or so. Mr. Neff pointed out some cool stuff as we drove, including a couple of geysers. Those are super-hot water sprays that shoot out of the ground. The most famous one is Old Faithful, but we didn't see that one from the road.

"We'll see it soon, though," Ms. Garrison promised. "I know Egg wouldn't miss the chance to photograph such a famous landmark!"

Egg nodded eagerly.

Soon the bus stopped. We all piled out. "We hike from here, gang," Mr. Neff said.

It was still pretty early in the morning, so it wasn't too hot yet. I was getting used to the weight of my backpack, too. Still, something was annoying me as we hiked.

Gum.

"Here we come, bears!" he shouted as we walked. He also rang that big bell of his over and over. It was some racket.

"I think every bear in the park knows you're here!" Cat said, giggling.

Egg sighed. He said, "I'll never get a good shot of any wildlife, never mind bears, with all this noise."

Gum kept ringing his bell. "Sorry, guys," he said. "As long as I'm in this park, I am going to make a lot of noise."

"Oh yeah?" I said. "What about when you're sleeping?"

Gum smiled. "Don't worry," he said. "I've got my radio. I'll just leave it on all night long."

"What?" I said. "How will we sleep?"

"Who can sleep with bears around?!" Gum said. "Honestly, Sam. Sometimes you make no sense to me." Then he went back to shouting.

I couldn't take it anymore, and neither could Cat. The two of us jogged ahead, toward the front of the group, just to get away from Gum's shouting.

Soon we reached a small clearing among tall pine trees. Beyond a small creek, the view was amazing. We saw tall, round mountains covered in green and white. I could hear a steady roar.

"What is that?" I asked Mr. Neff. "Are we near the freeway or something?"

He smiled at me. "No, Pam," he said. "That's a waterfall — Firehole Falls. We'll hike over there after lunch."

Egg and Gum walked up. Of course, with the way Gum was carrying on, I heard them before I saw them.

"Okay, bears," Gum shouted. "I'm going to set up a tent near here! So stay at least five miles from this spot until tomorrow night!"

"I don't think bears know miles," Gum said.

"Good point," Gum said. Then he shouted, "Stay eight kilometers away!"

Cat covered her eyes and shook her head.

"Gum," I said. I put my arm around his shoulders. "Sometimes it's hard to believe you solve crimes with us."

Suddenly, we heard yelling. "Drill, drill, drill!" shouted a man.

"Natural gas for America!" shouted a woman.

A small group of people approached the camp. They were all wearing the same T-shirt. It said, "Drill for Natural Gas!"

"What is this?" Mr. Neff asked.

The man at the front stopped. "Hello," he said. He smiled and held out a pamphlet. "Please take a pamphlet."

A woman stepped up next to him. "We're in the park today because Yellowstone is full of a great natural resource," she said. "Natural gas."

Ms. Garrison took a pamphlet. "The fuel?" she asked.

The man nodded. "That's right," he said. "And with the price of oil climbing, we need fuel right here in the United States."

"Can I have one of those?" Cat asked. The woman handed her a pamphlet.

Then a jeep rumbled right up to us and stopped. The air was full of dust for a moment. Two park rangers climbed out. They were not happy.

"There you are," one of them said. "You were instructed to leave the park. Now we're going to escort you out."

"You can't do this,"
the woman said.

"You need a permit to distribute literature in the park, ma'am," said the other ranger.

The man grabbed his pockets and patted his chest, like he was looking for something. "I'm sure I have it someplace," he said.

"We can take care of this at the main building," the ranger said.

"We'll have to collect the pamphlets you've given out at this site," the other ranger said. He faced Mr. Neff and Ms. Garrison. They handed him their pamphlets.

"Cat," I said, "let's hide, quick, so you don't have to give that back. Something weird is going on here."

She nodded, and the two of us ducked behind some bushes. Gum and Egg followed.

As we watched, another jeep rolled up. Three more rangers got out.

"Forget about these people for now," said one of the men. "We've got bigger trouble."

Cat dropped her pamphlet, and it glided out of the brush. One of the rangers put his big muddy boot right on it.

"Aw, nuts," Cat said.

I shushed her. I figured something big was going on if the rangers were letting the natural gas people go.

"What's the big deal?" asked one ranger.

"It's Superintendent Mulwray," said another ranger. "Actually it's her son, Hollis."

"What did he do now?" asked another ranger. "Just last week I had to get a team together to save a family of tourists he'd given bad directions to."

"This time it's Hollis himself who's in trouble," said a ranger. "He's been kidnapped."

Once the rangers left, the four of us crawled back to the campsite. One ranger was still there. He was talking to Mr. Neff and Ms. Garrison. "So, since you're with a bunch of children," he said, "park security has suggested we move you all to a campsite much closer to the main building."

Mr. Neff nodded. "Yes, that makes sense," he said.

Ms. Garrison shook her head and sniffled. "Oh, that poor boy," she said. "And his poor mother!"

Egg gave her a hug. "I'm sure he'll be okay, Mom," he said. But that just made Ms. Garrison cry harder.

"Okay, everyone," Mr. Neff said. "Gather around. The rangers are sending a few vans for us so we don't have to hike all the way back. They're going to drive us to a new campsite."

I grabbed Gum by the wrist. "I'm not going," I said quietly.

"What?" Gum said. "Why not?"

I pointed at the jeep nearby. "I bet they're heading to the crime scene," I said. "I'm going to go with them."

"You're nuts!" he said.

"If we don't get a look at the crime scene," I said, "how will we ever solve this crime?"

Gum looked worried.

"I'll be fine," I said. "Get going. I'll find you guys later."

I jogged over to the jeep, staying low so I wouldn't be spotted. I climbed in and ducked under a bunch of old blankets. Then the jeep rumbled off.

TRAPPED

The drive to Superintendent Mulwray's cabin took longer than I expected. We were practically back at the north entrance by the time we stopped.

I peeked out from under the blankets when the engine switched off. The place was crawling with park rangers and police officers.

As quietly as I could, I slipped off the back of the jeep. Then I hurried into the woods and ran around to the back of the house.

No one was around. I was able to go right up to the house and look in the windows. Inside, it looked normal. The TV was on. There was an open can of soda on the little table next to the couch. Only the coffee table — made of logs — was flipped over. I figured there'd been a struggle, but not much of one.

I crept along the back of the house, looking for any clues. Then I found something: broken glass. Above it, but higher than I could reach, was a smashed window.

"Right around this way, chief," came a booming voice. The investigators were heading my way. I ran quickly to the far side of the house.

"The superintendent is on her way here," said a different voice. More rangers and cops were coming from that way, too.

I was
trapped.

I had to think fast. First I licked my hands. Then I rubbed them on my face. Then I burst into tears. "Waah," I said. I can pretend to be a helpless girl if I have to. "Please help me!"

The rangers all rushed toward me. "I'm here with my school's nature club," I said. "I don't know where they are!" Then I started sobbing again.

"That's odd," one ranger said quietly. "That group is being driven to the campsite near the main building. How could she have gotten this far on her own?"

Before anyone could give that too much thought, I sobbed loudly. I wailed, "I want my mommy!"

"We'd better get this girl back to her group," said a ranger. They led me to a jeep, and soon we were bouncing along the trail toward the campsite.

"Oh, thank goodness," Ms. Garrison said when I hopped off the jeep. "We were worried sick, Sam!"

"She must have wandered off," said the ranger who'd driven the jeep. He frowned and added, "Although I can't imagine how she wandered so far."

Egg, Cat, and Gum stood nearby. I winked at them. They were waiting for my report, but it would have to wait a little longer — till we could talk in private.

Once the rangers had all left, Mr. Neff told us to get our tents set up. We all had four-person tents — perfect for me and my friends.

Once we got it set up — and also put up the bell that Gum insisted on — we all climbed inside. Time for an update.

"Foul play for sure," I said.

"What did you find at the cabin?" Egg asked.

I told them about the window and flipped table.

"Sounds like the kid tried to fight back," Gum said.

Someone giggled outside the tent. I jumped up and opened the flap. Anton was standing nearby with his two goons.

"Hey," I said.

I stomped over to them.

Anton and his friends looked up and saw me. "Get out of here, Archer," Anton said. "We're having a private conversation."

"What are you laughing about?" I asked. "Were you listening to us?"

"Like you dorks would ever say anything worth hearing," Anton said.

Then they walked off toward their own tent.

Back inside our tent, Gum chewed his gum thoughtfully. "I know you think I blame Anton for . . . well, for everything," he said. "But this time, all the signs point to Anton."

"What signs?" Cat asked.

"Well," said Gum, "the last person who saw the missing kid, as far as we know, was either his mom or Anton."

"Huh?" Egg said. "The last time we saw him he was screaming at his mom. What does Anton have to do with it?"

"Anton was heading toward the superintendent's office as we left, remember?" Gum said. "And then he was the last one to reach the bus. He almost missed it."

"I even took pictures of him," Egg said. He showed us the pictures on the camera's display screen.

There was Anton, totally out of breath, walking down the aisle of the bus to join his two friends.

"So what kept him at the main building so long?" I asked.

Gum shrugged. "Who knows," he said. "But it's starting to add up."

"You guys, Anton wouldn't kidnap someone," Cat said.

"Maybe not," I said, "but let's go talk to him."

Egg unzipped the tent flap and we climbed out. Just as we did, there was Egg's mom, standing in the middle of the campsite. She rang a big bell by shaking it up and down.

"Hey," I whispered to Gum, "I think Egg's mom has your bell!"

"Attention, everyone," Ms. Garrison called. The club members gathered around. Anton and his goons were the last ones out of their tent. They were snickering at each other like hyenas with a secret.

"I guess by now you've all heard the whispers," Ms. Garrison said. "It seems a boy has gone missing in the park. For the rest of our trip, until the boy is found, we will be staying close to the main building."

"Boring!" Anton shouted. His goons laughed.

Ms. Garrison nodded. "It isn't the camping trip we hoped for," she admitted. "But we have to keep you kids safe. Now, we're heading to the main building for lunch."

"What about the geysers?" Egg asked, raising his hand.

"And the waterfall that Mr. Neff promised we'd see?" I asked.

"We'll see all that and more," Egg's mom said, "once the boy has been found and we know it's safe to explore again." She paused, and added, "But if they don't find him within forty-eight hours, they'll close the park."

I gasped. We had to solve this crime — and fast — or the field trip was ruined!

The club hiked to the main building. This time Gum gave the shouting and bell-ringing a rest. I guess he figured we were close enough to civilization that he didn't need to worry about it.

That, and there was a whole lot of yelling going on up ahead anyway.

"These guys again," Gum muttered.

It was the pamphleteers, of course. Egg started snapping photos of the group.

"I wonder," I said. "Cat, let's go grab another pamphlet, before they get arrested or something."

She nodded, and the two of us hurried ahead, past Mr. Neff and Ms. Garrison.

"There go Kitten and Pam," Mr. Neff said, chuckling. "Those two are inseparable." I looked back just in time to see Egg's mom roll her eyes.

Cat and I reached the pamphleteers just as the rangers pulled up. But the leader of the pamphleteers ran and threw a huge handful of pamphlets into the air. The wind caught them, and they flew off in every direction like a flock of sparrows.

"Grab one!" Cat shouted to me. She knew I was the fastest sixth-grader in school.

I took off after the windswept pamphlets like a shot. By the time I grabbed a copy — one got stuck in a low branch of a pine tree — half the pamphleteers were in handcuffs.

"Wow," I said, running over to join Cat. Gum and Egg had caught up by then too.

Just then, Superintendent Mulwray came bursting out of the main building's front door.

"You can't do this!" a pamphleteer shouted at her. "We have our rights!"

"This is in very poor taste," Ms. Mulwray said, her face red. "My son is missing, possibly in serious danger, and you're harassing our visitors with these political attacks! The drilling permits will never be signed! Never!"

Then she stormed back into the building.
A hush fell over the crowd.

"Let me see that pamphlet," Cat said. She
scanned it quickly, then flipped it over and
looked at the back.

"Here's our new number-one suspect,"
she said, pointing at the words printed at
the bottom: Paid for by NatuPowerCo. "This
energy company did it."

OLD FAITHFUL

We wanted to keep investigating, but our club mates had other plans. They managed to convince Mr. Neff to find the bus driver and take us to Old Faithful.

Two ranger jeeps escorted the bus. Then four rangers walked with the nature club from the bus to the geyser.

And Gum clanged his bell the entire time. Seriously. The entire time.

Still, I'd say it was worth it.

"Old Faithful is so popular because it is possible to predict when it will erupt to within about ten minutes," the guide said.

"So when will it happen?" I asked.

The guide glanced at her watch. "I'd say it's due to erupt any second," she said. And just as she said that, it started.

It was amazing. The water shot over a hundred feet into the air in a huge frothy white plume. Egg snapped photo after photo.

After two minutes, the eruption was over, and it was time to get back on the bus.

The bus rumbled along, back toward our boring campsite near the parking lot at the main building.

My friends and I huddled together in the last row. "We need to question one of those pamphleteers," I said.

I explained to Gum and Egg that Cat and I thought the energy company had kidnapped the Mulwray kid.

"It's going to be tough to question them, isn't it?" Gum asked. "I mean, weren't all of the pamphleteers arrested and dragged out of the park?"

He was right. If there were no pamphleteers around, finding some good evidence would be tough.

I sighed. Maybe our field trip was doomed.

* * *

That night, I lay on my back near our tent, looking at the stars.

It was an amazing view, nothing like the sky back home. Here you could see every single speck of light in the galaxy.

My friends were nearby. Egg was snapping long-exposure night shots. Cat was lying down at my side. Gum was flipping through a comic book, holding his flashlight in one hand.

"It's nice to just relax," I said.

But I spoke too soon, because that moment something snapped in the woods behind our tent.

Cat sat up. "Did you hear that?" she whispered.

"It's a bear!" Gum said, jumping to his feet. "Everyone shout! Where's my bell?"

But it wasn't a bear. A shadowy figure darted into the camp, past our tent, and then out the other side. In the trail behind the figure were handfuls of pamphlets — about drilling for natural gas.

"It's one of them," I said.

I started running. I could just make out the figure in front of me in the dark.

The others couldn't keep up, but that didn't matter. I was fast enough. Soon I'd caught the sneak. She tripped on a root and tumbled into the grass.

"Gotcha," I said, standing over her.

"Don't hurt me!" she said. She put her hands over her face.

"I don't plan to," I said. Then I dropped to my knees next to her. "Why were you sneaking around?"

"What choice did I have?" she said. She sat up. She wasn't as old as the other pamphleteers I'd seen. She couldn't have been much older than eighteen. I figured she was still in high school. "Those rangers arrested my dad!"

"The pamphleteer leader was your father?" I asked.

"Yup," she said. "So I'm continuing his work. This natural gas stuff is super important to him. He quit his job just to come out here and hand out pamphlets."

"Wow," I said. "What about your mom?"

The girl pointed behind us, over her shoulder. "She's still at our camp, over there," she said.

She got up, and we walked toward a single large tent among a bunch of smaller ones.

"Everyone from the natural gas task force is camped right here," she explained. "Thanks for walking me home. This has been a tough couple of days."

"I can imagine," I said.

I waved, but I didn't leave. I stepped into the shadows and doubled back. I wasn't going to miss this chance to snoop around the task force's campsite.

And boy, did I find something good.

"Where did you go?" Cat asked. She was pretty mad. After all, I'd disappeared after that girl, and with a kidnapper (or a human-eating bear) on the loose, who wouldn't worry?

"Sorry, Cat," I said. "But I'm okay, and I caught the sneaky pamphleteer. She was actually very nice. I went back to her campsite with her."

I held up the little notebook I'd found in an empty tent at the task force site. "And I found this," I said.

Gum grabbed it and flipped through the pages. "Looks pretty boring," he said.

"Flip to the end," I said. "There's a newspaper clipping."

"It's about Superintendent Mulwray," Gum said. His eyes went wide. "It even mentions her son!"

I nodded. "Exactly," I said. "They were planning this kidnapping from the beginning, I bet."

"But why?" Egg asked. He snapped a picture of the article. Then Gum slipped it back into the book.

"Simple," I said. "Instead of a ransom, the task force will just demand that Ms. Mulwray open the park to drilling for gas."

Gum smiled. "You're a genius, Sam," he said.

"So what's our next move?" Egg said.

"Lights out, everyone!" shouted Mr. Neff. "Tomorrow will be a big day!"

"I guess our next move is sleeping," I said. "But if this is about drilling, the task force will go straight to Superintendent Mulwray with their demands. In the morning, we'll go straight to her, too."

DEMANDS

The next day, our first stop was to Ms. Mulwray's office.

We knocked at the open door. "Ms. Mulwray?" Cat said. "Um, we're from the nature club trip. We wanted to talk to you about your son, Hollis."

Ms. Mulwray turned in her chair and faced us. Her brow wrinkled with interest and concern. "Go on," she said.

"Well," Cat said, "we think we know who might have taken him."

"Who?" Ms. Mulwray asked. "How do you know?"

"We believe it's the natural gas task force,"
I said. "And we believe they will be calling
you soon to make their demands."

She nodded slowly. "Of course," she said.
"They want me to sign off on that drilling
request." She shook her head. "I don't have
that kind of power."

Just then, the phone rang. She scooped it
up. "Superintendent Mulwray," she said. Then
her face went white. It was the kidnappers.
"Who is this?" she said. "What do you want
with my son?" She listened. "I see," she said.
She shot us a quizzical look. "I — I think
that can be arranged. . . . Yes. . . . Of course.
Tonight at ten. I'll be there." She listened
some more. "No police," she said. "Of course.
I understand. . . . Can I speak to Hollis? Well,
is he okay? . . . Fine. Tonight in the clearing
behind the main building."

And she hung up.

"Well?" I said.

"Strangest thing," she said. "They only want five hundred dollars."

"Five hundred?" Gum said. "Are you sure they didn't say five hundred thousand? Or five million?"

Superintendent Mulwray shook her head. "I'm sure," she said. "They want five hundred dollars."

She leaned back in her chair and folded her hands. "I guess it's not the natural gas people after all, huh?" she said.

My friends and I left the office and walked slowly toward the building exit. I remembered the last time we'd done that — when Anton went rushing past us toward the office. He must have run into Hollis in the hallway.

And then it all clicked.

"We're going to that ransom drop tonight, guys," I said. "For once, Gum, you're right."

Gum looked shocked.

THE SCHEME

Of the four of us, only Gum fell asleep before the plan began to unfold. It was eleven thirty when I heard footsteps outside our tent.

"They're not being very careful," I whispered to Cat.

I nudged Gum. His snoring stopped with a sputter and a cough. "I'm awake, I'm awake!" he said as he sat up. "No bears!"

I smirked at him. Then the four of us quietly climbed out of our tent.

"Hold it," I whispered. "You three wait here. I'll be right back."

I crouched and crossed the campsite. Anton's tent was quiet, and the flap was closed. That didn't stop me. Carefully, I opened the flap.

There was Anton, with his back to the flap, looking at something in his lap.

"Hi, Gutman," I said. I put my hands on both his shoulders. He stiffened.

"What do you want?" he asked.

I looked over his shoulder. He was flipping through a catalog from the big computer store back home.

"Got something in mind?" I asked him. "Some video game you've had your eye on?"

"You better get out of our tent," he said.

"Or what?" I asked.
"You'll set your goons on me?
Oh wait, they're not even
here, are they?"

"They, um, went to the bathroom," he said.

I crossed my arms and smirked at him. "You're coming with me," I said.

"What?" he asked. "I am not!"

But I grabbed him by the collar and dragged him right out of the tent.

"You weren't planning to let your goons do all the work tonight, were you?" I asked.

I led him right to my friends, and the five of us headed to the clearing behind the main building.

Superintendent Mulwray was in the middle of the clearing. She was holding a briefcase, probably the ransom money.

Anton struggled, but I held his wrists. When he tried to shout, Gum put a hand over his mouth.

I scanned the area, hoping I'd spot some movement in the darkness. Finally the bushes across the clearing shook.

"There," I said. I grabbed Egg's hand. "Let's go."

Together, Egg and I snuck through the bushes and woods, all the way around the clearing.

When we were close, Egg and I froze. "Now, take some pictures, straight ahead."

He did. His flash went off a hundred times in a few seconds, lighting up the bushes in front of us and alerting everyone to our presence.

Shouting. People running around in the darkness. Superintendent Mulwray calling into the night, "Who's there? Hollis, is that you?"

Egg showed me the display of his camera. It was just what I expected: Anton's goons and Hollis, crouched together, laughing.

Yup, even Hollis was cracking up. He wasn't tied up. He wasn't scared or crying or hurt. He was laughing.

The goons took off, trying to get back to the campsite. But they ran right into Gum and Cat. Surprised, they fell on their butts and rolled right into the clearing.

They sat up at Ms. Mulwray's feet.

"What is this?" Ms. Mulwray shouted.

Hollis wasn't laughing anymore. I grabbed him by the wrist and led him into the clearing.

"I think your son has some explaining to do," I said.

The superintendent turned and saw Hollis. She ran to him and gave him a big hug. "Thank goodness you're okay!" she said.

"He's fine," I said. "But it's not that simple. Right, Egg?"

Egg held out his camera and showed Ms. Mulwray the photos from the bushes. "I don't understand," she said. "Who are these boys?" Then she glanced down at Anton's goons on the ground. "Hmm," she said, narrowing her eyes. "I think I'm beginning to understand."

Just then, Mr. Neff and Ms. Garrison walked into the clearing too. "We heard the ruckus," Mr. Neff said. "What's happened here?"

"It appears," Ms. Mulwray said as she grabbed her son by the top of his ear, "that my son wasn't kidnapped at all."

"That's right," Gum said. "It was just a scheme."

"But I don't think Hollis should take all the blame," I said. "Neither should these two goons. After all, it takes a special kind of mind to come up with a plan like this. Isn't that right, Anton?"

"It was your idea?" Ms. Mulwray asked Anton.

"I met your son yesterday morning, when we first arrived," he explained. "When he told me he was mad he didn't get that GameStation, I thought of a way he could get the money he needed to buy it himself."

"And a little extra for yourself, huh?" I said.

"Well," Anton said, "I thought I should get paid for my part of the work."

"How did you four figure this out?" Superintendent Mulwray asked me.

"I was stumped at first when the ransom request came," I said. "It was such a tiny amount for a real kidnapper to ask for. Then I remembered that broken glass at the scene. It was outside of the house, as if someone had broken the glass from the inside. Why would the kidnapper have done that?"

She shrugged.

"Simple," I said. "He wouldn't. But your son might have if he wanted it to seem like someone had broken in. Then it all made sense."

Mr. Neff scratched his head. "I don't know how to handle this," he said. "I only know you and your friends are in big trouble, Anton."

"I figured," Anton said, shrugging.

Ms. Mulwray bent down and picked up one of those pamphlets. The things must have blown all over the park! "Hollis," she said with her hands on her hips, "will clean up every pamphlet from here to Idaho."

Anton and his goons cackled.

"And you three will join him," Mr. Neff said.

They stopped cackling.

"I guess it's safe to camp anywhere in the park now, huh?" I said to Mr. Neff. "And to hike to the waterfall?"

He nodded. "I don't see why not," he said.

"I do," Gum said, his eyes wide. Then he pulled that bell from his belt and stomped around, clanking it and shouting, "Bears! We're really going hiking now! Please stay eight kilometers away at all times!"

literary news

MYSTERIOUS WRITER REVEALED!

Steve Brezenoff lives in St. Paul, Minnesota, with his wife, Beth, their son, Sam, and their small, smelly dog, Harry. Besides writing books, he enjoys playing video games, riding his bicycle, and helping middle-school students work on their writing skills. Steve's ideas almost always come to him in his dreams, so he does his best writing in his pajamas.

arts & entertainment

ARTIST IS KEY TO SOLVING MYSTERY, SAY POLICE

Marcos Calo lives happily in A Coruña, Spain, with his wife, Patricia (who is also an illustrator), and their daughter, Claudia. When Marcos and Patricia aren't drawing, they like to go on long walks by the sea. They also watch a lot of films and eat Nutella sandwiches. Yum!

A Detective's Dictionary

encounter (en-KOUN-tur)–an unexpected meeting

erupt (i-RUHPT)–eject something at great force

foul play (FOUL PLAY)–unlawful or dishonest behavior

geyser (GYE-zur)–a hole in the ground through which hot water and steam shoot up in bursts

investigate (in-VESS-tuh-gayt)–find out as much as possible about something

kilometer (kuh-LOM-uh-tur)–a unit of length in the metric system equal to 1,000 meters, or about 0.6 miles

landmark (LAND-mark)–an important place or building

pamphlet (PAM-flit)–a small booklet that includes information on one particular topic

permit (PUR-mit)–a written statement giving permission for something

ransom (RAN-suhm)–money that is demanded in return for someone who is being held captive

resource (REE-sorss)–something valuable or useful

scheme (SKEEM)–plan

Sam Archer

Nature Club

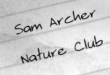

Ⓐ

Yellowstone National Park

The 3,472 square miles that make up Yellowstone National Park cover land in three states and include forest, grasslands, and water. The national park was established by President Ulysses S. Grant in 1872 and was the world's first national park.

Yellowstone National Park has more than three hundred geysers, but the most famous is, of course, Old Faithful. Yellowstone is also home to an active volcano, which is monitored around the clock by scientists. Most experts think that the Yellowstone Volcano will not erupt in the next thousand years. Old Faithful, though, erupts every day!

In fact, Old Faithful erupts every hour to 90 minutes. Viewers can predict the next eruption within about ten minutes of the actual time based on the length of the previous eruption.

According to some sources, Old Faithful isn't just a tourist site – it has been used as a laundry! Clothes placed inside the geyser would shoot up with the eruption and fall down clean. I don't think that's something I'll try if I ever get to travel there again!

Pam – wonderful work! I hope we can visit again. I'd like to try that laundry trick! – Mr. N

FURTHER INVESTIGATIONS

CASE #FTMI3SAYNP

1. In this book, the Nature Club (including me) went on a field trip. What field trips have you gone on? Which one was your favorite, and why?

2. If you went on a field trip to Yellowstone, what would you be most excited to see? Talk about your answer.

3. Who else could have been a suspect in this mystery?

IN YOUR OWN DETECTIVE'S NOTEBOOK . . .

1. Write about a time you got into trouble. What happened? How do you feel about it now?

2. Sam, Cat, Gum, and Egg are best friends. Write about your best friend.

3. This book is a mystery story. Write your own mystery story!

THEY SOLVE CRIMES, CATCH CROOKS, CRACK CODES, ... AND RIDE THE BUS BACK TO SCHOOL AFTERWARD.

Meet Egg, Gum, Sam, and Cat. Four sixth-grade detectives and best friends. Wherever field trips take them, mysteries aren't far behind!

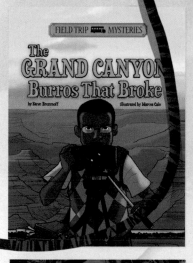

FIELD TRIP MYSTERIES

The
GRAND CANYON
Burros That Broke

by Steve Brezenoff   Illustrated by Marcos Calo

FIELD TRIP MYSTERIES

The
Mount RUSHMORE
Face That
Couldn't See

by Steve Brezenoff   illustrated by Marcos Calo

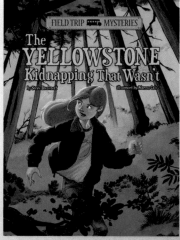

FIELD TRIP MYSTERIES

The
YELLOWSTONE
Kidnapping That Wasn't

by Steve Brezenoff   illustrated by Marcos Calo

FIELD TRIP MYSTERIES

The
EVERGLADES
Poacher Who Pretended

by Steve Brezenoff   illustrated by Marcos Calo

4
New
Mysteries